BARBARA HELEN BERGER

A Lot of Otters

PHILOMEL BOOKS ✳ NEW YORK

Mother Moon
was looking for her child.
"Where is my moonlet?
Where is—"

Oops.

Mother Moon
was looking for her child.
"Where is my moonlet?
Where is my little one?"

She called and called.
She cried and cried.
With every tear
that fell from her eyes,
a star fell into the sea.

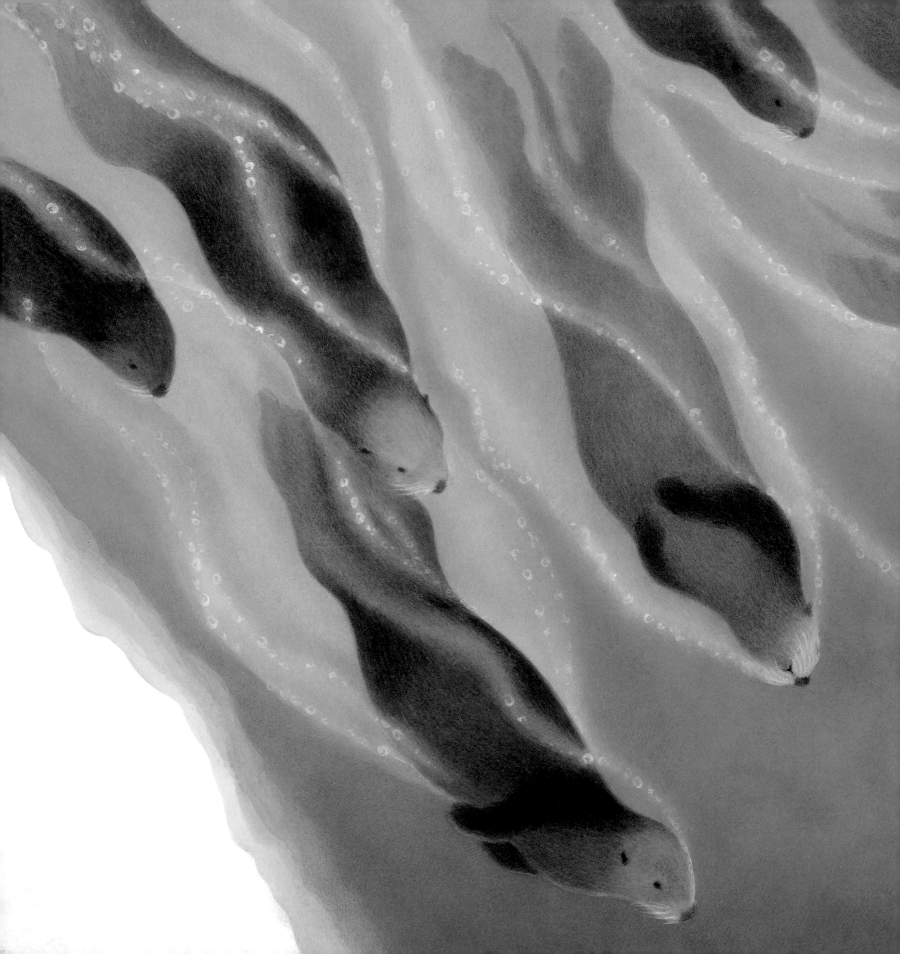

A lot of otters
saw the stars fall.
They dove down
into the dark,

down into the deep.

They carried the stars
up to the top of the sea.

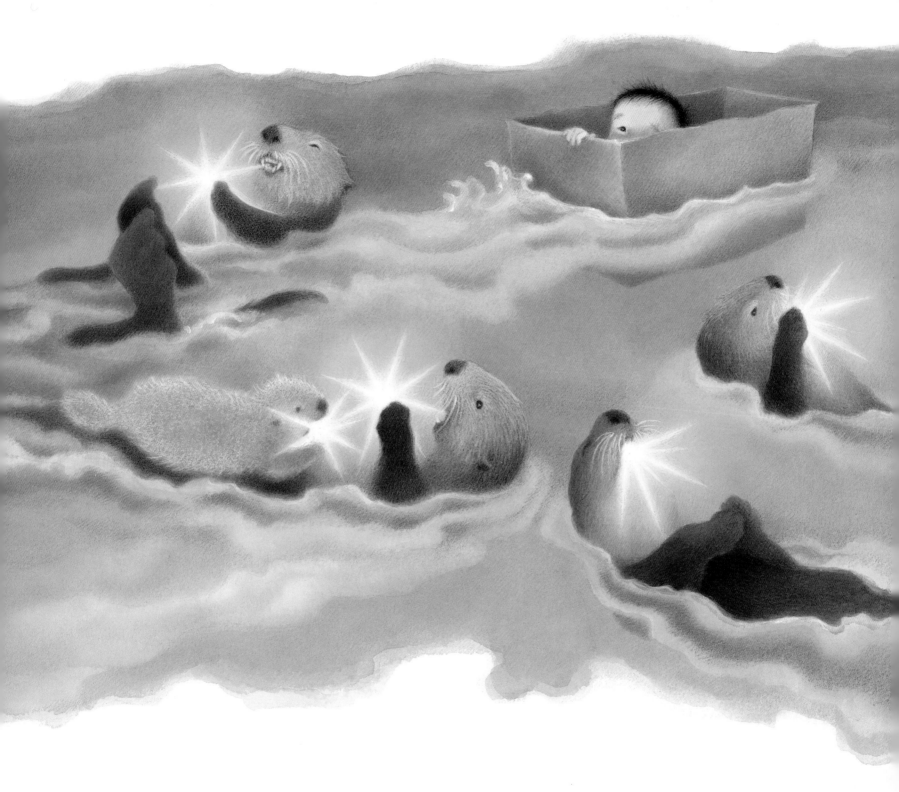

The otters tasted the stars.

They wrestled and rolled
and rubbed the starlight
into their fur.

They bobbed and cavorted
and rollicked around.
They made
such a commotion of light
that Mother Moon
looked down.

"Moonlet? My little one?"
She came running out of the clouds,
over the dark, over the deep.

There
she found her child,
safe with a lot of otters

in a sea of stars.

To Pat

Patricia Lee Gauch, Editor

Text and illustrations copyright © 1997 by Barbara Helen Berger
All rights reserved. This book, or parts thereof, may not be reproduced
in any form without permission in writing from the publisher,
Philomel Books, 200 Madison Avenue, New York, NY 10016. Philomel Books,
Reg. U.S. Pat. & Tm. Off. Published simultaneously in Canada.
Printed in Hong Kong by South China Printing Co. (1988) Ltd.
Book design by Donna Mark and Barbara Helen Berger.
The text is set in Garamond Light.
Library of Congress Cataloging-in-Publication Data
Berger, Barbara. A lot of otters / Barbara Helen Berger. p. cm.
Summary: As a lot of otters wrestle, roll, and cavort on the water,
they make such a commotion of light that Mother Moon finds her lost child.
[1. Lost children—Fiction. 2. Otters—Fiction. 3. Moon—Fiction.] I. Title.
PZ7.B4513Lo 1997 [E]—DC20 95-50532 CIP AC
ISBN 0-399-22910-8
3   5   7   9   10   8   6   4